Keepers of the House

KEEPERS OF THE HOUSE

by
George
Mackay Brown

illustrated
by
Gillian Martin

The Old Stile Press

First published in 1986 by The Old Stile Press

Published in this edition in 1987
by Impact Books, 112 Bolingbroke Grove,
London SW11 1DA

Text © George Mackay Brown 1986
Pictures © The Old Stile Press 1986

British Library Cataloguing in Publication Data
Brown, George Mackay
    Keepers of the house.
    I. Title   II. Martin, Gillian, *1959-*
    823'.914[F]   PR6Q41.R59

    ISBN 0-245-54608-1

Contents

Firekin

Firekin is the name of the guardian
who lives in the chimney. Firekin
says to the birds on the roof, 'Better
not try to build a nest in the chimney or you'll get burnt.' Firekin
pushes the smoke out. On a winter
night, when mother is having guests,
Firekin has his work cut out to push
all that coal smoke out under the
stars. He grunts and groans, and
sometimes a stray flame licks his
ankle, and by the time all the guests
have gone Firekin is as black as
midnight at the North Cape on the
winter solstice. But sometimes Firekin has an easy job, for example on
a summer afternoon when everyone
is out in the garden sunbathing or
seeing to the flowers. Then Firekin
sits half-way up the chimney and

snoozes. In the summer he gets very fat and lazy. One summer morning Firekin got a right fright. Mother had sent for the sweep. Firekin was snoozing half-way up the chimney when a hard brush hit him, three or four times. He was knocked half-stupid. He had the sense to fly out of the chimney and he went, mauled and zig-zag, to visit his friend Firebald in Mrs Mitchell's chimney. Firekin and Firebald hadn't seen each other for a year. They had lots of news to exchange. Firekin inspected Firebald's chimney. He thought it wasn't nearly so nice and black and scorched as his own. But he said nothing. At last a starling shouted down Firebald's chimney, 'Tell Firekin he can come out now! The sweep's away.' At once Firekin, with a whirr, was back in his own swept chimney.

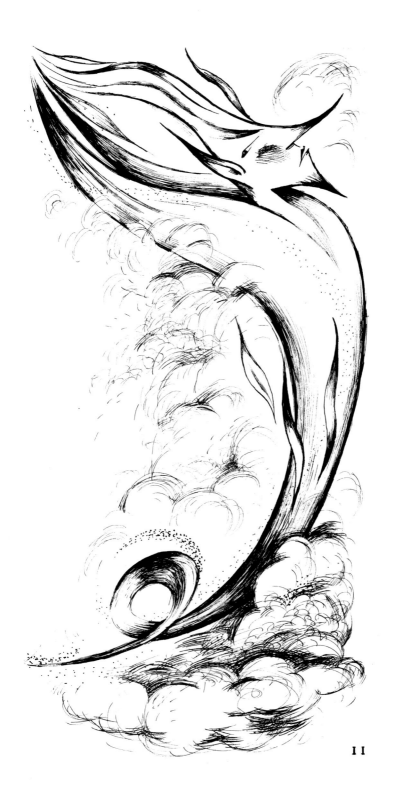

II

Windhove

Windhove is the name of the guardian who lives in the window. You can't see Windhove, he's clearer than the glass itself. Windhove likes to sit half-way up near the window-latch. With one eye he watches the birds, cats, cars, people on the street outside. With his other eye he watches the goings-on inside the house: Willie sleeping in the crib, mother making apple-pie, Smitch the cat licking his paw outside the mouse-hole, the spider in the centre of his web in the corner. One day a sparrow came and sat on the window-sill. He pecked at the pane with his beak. 'What do you want?' said Windhove to the sparrow. 'Mind what you're doing, there's a good bird.' The sparrow said to Windhove, 'It's that spider inside. Be my friend. I'd like him for my dinner.' 'I have no objection to that,' said Windhove. 'Wait till the woman of the house opens the lower sash to shake her duster. Then fly in and do what you have to do.' ... So when mother was shaking hairs and specks of dust and breadcrumbs and pussy-fur out of her duster into the wind, the sparrow flew in. What a commotion there was in that house for five minutes! The sparrow went for the spider (who at that very moment was eyeing a fly buzzing round his web). The cat leapt at the sparrow and just missed, but leapt again, three or four times. Little Willie began to yell in the crib. Mother cried from the window, 'What on earth's going on?' 'Quick,' sang Windhove in his inaudible voice to the sparrow. 'Fly out quick now!' The sparrow did just that. The cat Smitch leapt after the sparrow and ended up in the gooseberry bush below. Mother put a piece of fudge in Willie's mouth and he stopped crying. 'Oh dear,' said Windhove to himself, 'I have caused a commotion! I'll be good for the rest of the day. I'll say to the raincloud, "Send rain to wash the window." I'll say to the east wind, "Dry it fast." I'll say to the boy throwing stones, "If you don't stop that, I'll fly at you and give you a draught in the eye. I don't want any showers of glass in this house."

Jambone

Jambone is the name of the guardian who looks after the cupboard.
Jambone whispers in mother's ear,
'Shopping day today, Mrs Moness.
There's only a little pat of butter left.
The sugar's low in the jar. You need
a loaf - Jennifer had her friends in
last night when you were out and
they cut six slices to make toast. Cat-
food for Smitch. What about honey?
- you haven't had honey for a whole
year.' So Jambone is a good friend
to the family. One winter Jambone
tasted so much stuff out of the cupboard - a little bit of this and a little
spread of that and a little crumb of
the other - he grew very very fat and
lazy. He slept and drowsed most of
the time, and scratched his round
tummy. He would forget to whisper

to mother what was needed for the cupboard, so that mother (who of course had no idea that Jambone existed - nor does anybody else except you and me) kept complaining, 'How forgetful I am these days! I'm buying in all the wrong things from the shops. Last Friday I bought a pound of ham when I already had a pound and a half in the larder . . . Yesterday I forgot to buy marmalade, though I knew there had been no marmalade for three breakfasts, and father was in a bad mood because he likes marmalade so much. Oh dear, oh dear, this will never do!' . . . One day, after sampling some gooseberry jam, a bit of cheese, and three sugar cubes, Jambone happened to see himself reflected in the glass of the jam-jar. His cheeks were bursting! His eyes were popping! He had seven chins! His knuckles were all dimples-in-fat! He said, 'How gross and ugly I look! No wonder the lady of the house is buying in all the wrong things. I must take a tumble to myself. I'll be good and attend to my duties from now on.' . . . So Jambone went on a strict diet, and he began once more to keep exact accounts of all the goods in the cupboard, and whisper to mother - who was unaware of him, of course - what was needed when she was buttoning up her coat to go out shopping. . . . That family, I'm telling you - and who are you to deny it - ate the most balanced diet, with just the right amount of vitamins and carbo-hydrates, in the entire town.

Thanks to Jambone, who is now as thin as a stalk of rhubarb.

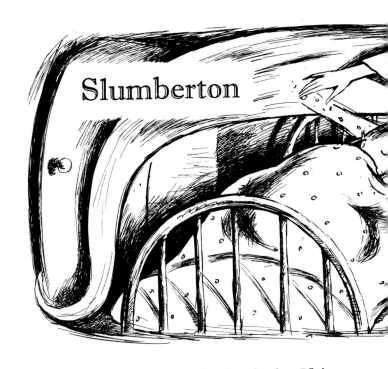

Slumberton

Slumberton guards the beds. If it wasn't for Slumberton we would hardly get a wink of sleep. Did you know we all turn a number of times in the night? Well, we do. Slumberton keeps us from being bound in bed-clothes like Egyptian mummies. How would you like a spider to drop into your open slumbering mouth and spin a web in your throat? Slumberton sees that that doesn't happen, or only once in a century. Slumberton has a busy night of it,

from bed-time to breakfast-time. If he sees a mouse nibbling at the bed-side candle, he hauls it off by the scruff of its neck. If - as sometimes happens - Jennifer has a nightmare, shivering and shrieking in her dreadful sleep, Slumberton shakes her awake gently. Slumberton whispers in her ear that it was all a silly dream - she is really a happy carefree schoolgirl! Slumberton has had a busy time ever since little Willie was born. Willie sleeps most of the time, and so Slumberton has to be on almost constant duty. But Slumberton doesn't mind that - the sight of such innocence asleep in the crib is compensation enough. Only once has Slumberton let that household down. That was when Mr Moness - Jennifer's and Willie's father - took a hot-water bottle to bed with him one night in winter. Slumberton ought to have seen to it that the stopper was securely turned. But that night - owing to Willie having been teething for three bawling whimpering days - Slumberton dropped off to sleep on the eleventh step of the stairway. He was wakened by a fearful yell, a blacker more powerful yell than anything little Willie could dredge up! Mr Moness's feet had been scalded. Mr Moness had to have the doctor. He was off work for a week. The best night of the year for Slumberton is when Santa Claus comes. Slumberton is the first to welcome Santa as he eases himself down the chimney, and pulls his bag of gifts after him. Slumberton brushes pieces of soot off Santa's red robe. (He has seen to it, of course, that the fire in the grate is well and truly out - no burnt feet for Santa!) Santa and Slumberton shake hands warmly. They have known each other for a very long time. Slumberton takes Santa by the arm and leads him to the table where Jennifer has laid out a slice of cake and a glass of sherry. 'Ah,' says Santa every year, 'I needed that!' Then Slumberton precedes Santa to the foot of the stairs, and bows politely, indicating the way to the children's bedroom. . . . It is Slumberton who shouts to the moon-tranced cats in the garden below, 'Here, cut out that row! Some folk in here are trying to sleep! Away with you, or I'll see to it you don't get another drop of milk at this house.' . . . Then the cats take their mad fiddles away to some other garden.

Tulirosanthemus

Tulirosanthemus is the name of the
garden gnome. (He's the only keeper
of the house you can actually see.)
You might think he does nothing
but crouch there all the round year.
You would be quite wrong. Tulirosanthemus - in future I'm going to
call him just T, it's such a sweat
writing out his name time after time
- well, in winter T growls, 'Get up,
snowdrops! What's wrong with you?
Don't you want to see the last of
your sister, the snow? She's very ill,
the snow. She's fading away.' Then
the snowdrops come out, and put
sad drooping white looks on their
dying sister. In spring it's,' Come on,
grass! Stir yourselves. Be a green
army marching towards the gold
castle of summer.' And the grasses

unsheath their green swords and
march towards the sun. So it goes
on, all the year round. He has a very
harsh grating voice, T. Well, you'd
know that, wouldn't you, by the
awkward look on his face. 'Come on,
daffodils - what do you think you
got golden trumpets for? Blow them.
Spring is here. The primroses have
beaten you to it, you slugabeds!
Primroses are all along the banks of
the burn.' . . . 'Oh,' sneers T sar-
castically, 'have the high and mighty
roses deigned to honour our garden
at last? Welcome, beauteous fair
ladies. Let me tell you, however,
Mrs Moness is of the opinion that
tulips are better than you any day.
She always has a bowl of tulips in
the living room. So there!' At that
one of the roses flushes, another
grows pale, another drops a tear. (It
required the repeated praise of the
blackbird to reassure the insulted
rosebush.) 'Ready for a battle, are
you, grassblades,' sniggered T one

evening. 'Brave soldiers, marching to the bright fortress of the sun, prepare yourselves for battle.' For T has seen Mr Moness coming out of the garden shed with the lawn-mower. It was a terrible battle while it lasted. The grass was decimated, ruthlessly and systematically. Their beautiful green swords were broken and strewn here and there. Only a few stragglers were left at the end of that terrible evening, but not for long - Mrs Moness's garden shears put paid to the stragglers. But never think the grass nation was conquered. Again and again, as summer advanced, they summoned up new hosts and marched towards the sun. Millions died in that garden war . . . 'You clear off!' snarled T suddenly to an intruding blackbird. 'This garden belongs to Jet the blackbird and Sloe his wife. Can't you see their nest in the tree there?' 'O tree,' sighs T, 'you're getting old, not such good leafage on your branches as there was last year!' Tree creaks and groans, it would love to take that evil T in its leafy hands and strangle him. So the flowers come and go all summer long, summoned and despatched by T. 'Daisies, idiots!' he yells. 'Will you never learn? Come to make the lawn beautiful, have you, with your thousand stars? You'd have been better, I'm telling you, in a ditch, shining for some tramp that's stopped there to eat his crust. For this again is the evening of the lawn-mower.' Sure enough, a thousand stars were torn from their green firmament by the clanking jaws of the lawn-mower, before dark. 'You slimy worms, I hate you!' shrills T. Another time he chortles, 'Worms, beware of blackbird!' Jet comes and pulls bits of long wet rubber out of the lawn. The days get shorter. Jennifer wears her muffler and woollen gloves to school. 'I'm sick and tired of all living things,' says T on dark stormy days.

'Away with you! Can't I have any peace? You miserable - looking bunch!' Later, a little cold white moth drifts on to T's nose. 'You've come at last, snow,' says T. 'Now I can have a rest.' The white moths tumbled and trembled and curtained down in millions and billions and trillions. The garden was no more. It was wiped out, cancelled, a blank. And T nodded on his pedestal, the windward side of him sheathed in snow, and had a long white dream. Once he opened one eye - it was the middle of January - and saw an intruder in the garden, a thick white inane-looking fellow with a cold pipe in his mouth, red buttons down his front, a torn fair-isle scarf wound about where a neck should have been. 'You scum!' snarled T. Jennifer's face was two apples and two stars and a winter rose. 'Blast it!' grumbled T; and went off to sleep for a few weeks more.

Yearpang

The name of the guardian who looks after time in the house is Yearpang. If it wasn't for Yearpang there would be no sense or order in the house. It is Yearpang more than hunger that makes Willie yell for his bottle. It's Yearpang who causes mother to cry out, 'O dear, Sidney will be home from the office in ten minutes, and I haven't got the tatties on!' Yearpang sits inside the grandfather clock; he likes to leap on to the brass pendulum and swing back and fore, back and fore. The only things he reads are calendars, year books, and old diaries. He is very officious whenever a leap-year falls; he likes the extra work; he whispers in Jennifer's ear, 'Twenty-nine days in February this year,' and then Jennifer shouts

out in the middle of the meal,
'Mama, this is a leap-year!' And
mother answers mildly, 'Well, well,
I know.' And Mr Moness says, 'Eat
your clapshot and sausage, girl, stop
chattering.' And little Willie pulls
himself up in his crib and wonders
what it's all about. Often Yearpang
sits among the chimneys and watches
the sun from its rising to its setting.
'Another day,' he says. He makes a
tick in his account book, and climbs
down to spend the night inside the
grandfather clock. Not every night,
though. Three nights a month (sup-
posing there's a clear sky) Yearpang
climbs to his observation post among
the chimney-pots. Once, when the
moon is a new silver gondola. Again,
when the moon is a fat Chinaman
blandly admiring himself in the sea.
Again, when the moon is a cold
cinder crumbling into last gray ash.
'Moon,' says Yearpang when the sky
belongs only to the stars again,
'moon, you are the greatest actor in

the sky!' When it is midsummer, the longest day, at noon Yearpang peers from behind the curtain at all the cheerful sunsmitten folk going past on the street. 'Go on, fools,' he says, 'behave as if all time was before you.' At midwinter, he says to mother, 'Don't be so worried, woman. This is the worst. Everything will get brighter after today, believe me.' And at once Mrs Moness cheers up, and puts an extra spoon of tea in the teapot. In March and in September, at the equinoxes, when day and night are equal, Yearpang goes down at noon into the garden. He stands facing the sun, he turns, one half of him bright, one half dark. Yearpang says, some nights when he can't get to sleep, 'I was here when they laid the foundation stone of this house. It seems like yesterday. I'll still be here in three hundred years' time when there'll only be myself, spiders, rats, fallen beams. That day, I'll only have one more white hair and one more wrinkle on my brow. How I'll miss Jennifer and Willie! I mind all the other bairns that grew up here and went away and never came back. There'll be more generations of children to come, of course. Once there was a baby in this house - oh, a hundred years ago - and I saw him growing into a greedy mischievous boy, then into a youth who liked boats and horses and girls, then into a sailor that sailed away and came back again and again and again, then into a father with a handsome black beard and a bronze watch chain across his stomach, smelling of cloves and coffee, for he bought a shop at last with his sea-money; then into an old man who sat in the corner and told lies to the cat and the canary (for in the end nobody else would listen), then into a long silent shrouded man. He was out of my keeping then' . . . Sometimes Year-pang sighs, 'Oh dear, the same thing, over and over again. Little Willie over there in the crib, he hardly lasts longer than a snowflake. When will I get some rest?' Then he leaps on to the pendulum of the grandfather clock, and rides through the night to welcome in the new shy primrose-with-promise day.

Badmerry

Badmerry is the wicked spirit - you could hardly call him a guardian - who makes all the mischief in the house. 'Where did I put that needle!' Mrs Moness complains. 'Father needs that button in his shirt for tonight's council meeting.' Then Badmerry sits in the corner and picks his nose and sniggers. 'This cheese, it's gone off!' cries the lady of the house from the kitchen, when everyone is wanting to have cheese and biscuits and cocoa for supper. Badmerry, sitting invisible on top of the cooker, can hardly contain himself. It was Badmerry who touched the cheese with a finger of decay. 'If that isn't too bad!' laments Mrs Moness. 'I paid that piano-tuner ten pounds not a year ago. Just listen to it! Jennifer

will ruin her ear, and her so pro-
mising, Miss Willkie the music
teacher says.' Badmerry wheezes
with mirth; he has been among the
strings all morning. One day Mrs
Moness noticed a patch of damp on
the bedroom ceiling. Father said
they'd better get the builder in.
Along came the builder three days
later. He climbed the stair, puffing
and coughing. He examined the
damp patch with a sagacious eye.
He said, 'It's nothing. I'm very busy.
It's just a stray drop of rain. Don't
worry.' (Later he sent in a bill for
five pounds, in consideration of his
expert opinion.) Badmerry heard all
this, sitting on a rafter in the attic.
His eyes were slits of delight. Just
after the builder left, grunting his
way downstairs, Badmerry stood on
the beam and stretched himself full
length and yanked another roof
slate out of place. 'Rain, come
quickly!' whispered Badmerry. I
don't know whether or not the rain

listens to creatures like Badmerry - I doubt it - but it so happened that the rain fell for three nights and three days incessantly the following week. The damp patch, which had looked in the beginning like the map of a gray little island - possibly one of the Hebrides - grew and grew. At the end of the third day's rain it was a vast continent that covered a quarter of the bedroom ceiling. While Mr Moness slept one night, a drop of water fell from the ceiling into his open blissfully sleeping mouth, and jerked him all at once into the harsh real world of dampness and decay. Once more the builder grumphed and thundered his way upstairs. He set his sad eye on the growing continent of wetness. He pursed his lips. He nodded wisely. He tilted his head. He ordered his apprentice to set a ladder between bedroom and attic. The woodwork creaked under his huge ascending bulk. He disappeared through the trapdoor.

They heard him sighing and stumbling in the torch-shot darkness above. He descended after ten minutes. He said hopelessly to Mr Moness, 'Roof's rotten. Don't know when I can do it, so many things to do. Difficult to get slates. Anyway, you need a new roof before winter.' The new roof was on before winter, and it cost Mr Moness one thousand pounds! Not to speak of all the dust and discomfort throughout the house. It was the merriest month in Badmerry's whole life. While the old slates fell in cascades, he would be convulsed with helpless mirth, sitting unseen on Mrs Mitchell's roof opposite, in order to get a better view of the chaos. When Mr Moness dolefully signed the £1000 cheque, Badmerry thought he would burst himself. To celebrate, he put a stye in Jennifer's left eye (which meant that she couldn't play the piano at the school concert). He dropped a penny into the washing machine so that it wouldn't work. 'More expense!' lamented Mrs Moness. He gave the baby a gripe one afternoon when the minister was visiting. 'Really,' said Badmerry to himself, 'I lead a rich and satisfying life.' He wandered down to the garden and carefully put a greenfly grub into the rosebush, under the baleful glare of Tulirosanthemus the gnome. Then he picked his nose and wondered what fun he would have next.

from
The Old Stile Press

Keepers of the House was written
in 1976 but was first published in
a hand-printed edition limited to
225 copies, in March 1986, by
Frances and Nicolas McDowall at
The Old Stile Press,
Catchmays Court, Llandogo,
Nr Monmouth, Gwent NP5 4TN.
Details of Old Stile Press editions
can be obtained from this address.